Can I Bring Saber to New York City, Ms. Mayor?

Lois G. Grambling

Illustrated by Judy Love

Charlesbridge

To Jeffrey Arthur, our son, and to Jeffrey Anthony, our great-grandson.
—L. G. G.

For Sue, my dear friend and NYC liaison, with gratitude for your voice of reason.
For Roger, my constant companion, whose love and encouragement spur me on.
And a big thank-you to Lisa, my mayoral muse: your spirit inspires me.
—J. L.

Text copyright © 2014 by Lois G. Grambling
Illustrations copyright © 2014 by Judy Love
All rights reserved, including the right of reproduction in whole or in part in any form.
Charlesbridge and colophon are registered trademarks of Charlesbridge Publishing, Inc.

Published by Charlesbridge
85 Main Street
Watertown, MA 02472
(617) 926-0329
www.charlesbridge.com

Library of Congress Cataloging-in-Publication Data
Grambling, Lois G.
    Can I bring Saber to New York City, Ms. Mayor? / Lois G. Grambling ; illustrated by Judy Love.
        p. cm.
    Summary: A boy wants to take Saber, a saber-toothed tiger, on a class trip to New York City to see the sights.
    ISBN 978-1-58089-570-5 (reinforced for library use)
    ISBN 978-1-58089-571-2 (softcover)
    ISBN 978-1-60734-743-9 (ebook)
    ISBN 978-1-60734-639-5 (ebook pdf)
1. Saber-toothed tigers—Juvenile fiction. 2. School field trips—Juvenile fiction. 3. New York (N.Y.)—
Description and travel—Juvenile fiction. [1. Saber-toothed tigers—Fiction. 2. School field trips—Fiction.
3. New York (N.Y.)—Description and travel—Fiction.] I. Love, Judith DuFour, illustrator. II. Title.
PZ7.G7655Caj 2014
813.54—dc23   2013014222

Printed in China
(hc) 10 9 8 7 6 5 4 3 2 1
(sc) 10 9 8 7 6 5 4 3 2 1

Illustrations done on Strathmore Series 500 Bristol with black ink and transparent dyes
Display type set in Big Limbo by Bitstream Inc.
Text type set in Tempus Sans by Galapagos Design Group Inc.
Color separations by KHL Chroma Graphics, Singapore
Printed and bound February 2014 by Jade Productions in Heyuan, Guangdong, China
Production supervision by Brian G. Walker
Designed by Diane M. Earley

If I brought Saber to New York City on our class trip,
we'd visit the 151-foot-tall Statue of Liberty,
the symbol of our freedom
and one of the most famous women in America.

Saber knows it must be tough
working for such a bustling city, Ms. Mayor,
so he'd be happy to help you
and Lady Liberty
greet all the visitors at the statue.

He'd rub against people's legs
and purr.
I'm sure everyone
would understand that
this is a cat's way of saying,
"WELCOME!"

Can I bring Saber to New York City, Ms. Mayor?

Can I?

PLEASE?!

If I brought Saber to New York City,
he'd head straight for the observation deck
of the Empire State Building.
Cats love to climb,
so up he'd go,
just like King Kong.
Then he'd look over the city
and roar a friendly hello
to all the pedestrians below.

Saber may be great at climbing up
the Empire State Building,
but he's a big SCAREDY-CAT
when it comes to taking
the express elevator down.
Don't worry, though.
You and the entire class
would help Saber make it
down all 102 floors, Ms. Mayor.

Can I bring Saber to New York City, Ms. Mayor?

Can I?

PLEASE?!

If I brought Saber to New York City,
he'd want to go to Lincoln Center
to see the Metropolitan Opera.
If one of the singers lost his voice,
Saber could fill in.
He has purr-fect pitch,
and his sharp canine teeth
would hardly interfere
with the performance.

Saber would steal the show.
Afterward, Ms. Mayor,
you and the conductor
would surely want
Saber the Singing Cat
to perform every night.

If I brought Saber to New York City,
he'd love strolling through Times Square
to take in all the sights
and watch all the people.

Can I bring Saber to New York City, Ms. Mayor?

Can I?

PLEASE?!

If I brought Saber to New York City,
he'd want to ride on the subway.
It'd be the first time Saber went underground
on a fast train.

Saber would hold the doors for rushing commuters
and let those who couldn't reach the subway handles
hang on to him.

Can I bring Saber to
New York City, Ms. Mayor?

Can I?

PLEASE?!

The subway would take Saber to Yankee Stadium.
He'd see his favorite baseball team play the Detroit Tigers,
which would be doubly exciting
because Saber is sometimes called
a tiger, too!

When the Yankees would get up to bat,
he'd wear his Yankees cap and shirt
and root for the home team.
And when the Tigers would get up to bat,
he'd wear a Tigers cap and shirt
and howl for the visiting team.
Saber would be a happy fan
no matter which team won.

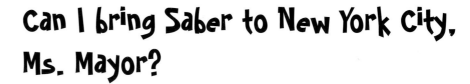

**Can I bring Saber to New York City,
Ms. Mayor?**

Can I?

PLEASE?!

If I brought Saber to New York City,
he'd get awfully hungry.
At the nearest hot dog stand,
he'd order four hot dogs:
one with mustard,
one with ketchup,
one with sauerkraut,
and one with EVERYTHING.
(He's no kitten!)

He'd wash them down with
some warm milk and lick his paws clean.
(Well, maybe he's a bit like a kitten.)
Every hot dog vendor in the city
would love to serve Saber.

If I brought Saber to New York City,
he'd want to go to the Central Park Zoo.
Saber would get to know the animals so well,
he'd become the best tour guide in the entire zoo.
You'd be so proud, Ms. Mayor.

At the zoo we would throw Saber a party.
Everyone would have a rattling good time.
Saber would
CHAT
with the parrots and
LOUNGE
with the lizards.

He'd stay cool with the polar bear.
Of course there would be DANCING, too!

Can I bring Saber to New York City, Ms. Mayor?

Can I?

PLEASE?!

After the party
Saber would want to find a cozy place to rest.
Central Park's Alice in Wonderland statue
would be just the spot.
What better place to take a catnap
than curled up in Alice's lap?

And, Ms. Mayor,
you could help Saber fall asleep
by reading to him
under the city's skyline.

Oh, dear, Ms. Mayor.
I'm afraid trying to nap in New York City
would be too loud and noisy for Saber.
He would be reminded of
his catnaps at home.
Saber would want to travel back to
his quiet neighborhood
in the peaceful countryside.
I guess Saber is really too much of
a homebody to visit New York City.
But don't worry.
He has another friend
who loves city adventures.
So . . .

Can I bring Sloth to New York City, Ms. Mayor?

Can I?

PLEASE?!